MW01230319

Winter
Wonderland

Books and stories by T. Lee Harris

Twenty-Seven Cents of Luck (Short)
Cat in the Middle (Short)
Sweet Water From the Rock (Short)
Muddy Waters (Short)
Winter Wonderland (Novella)

In the Miller and Peale Series
San Francisco at Night (Short)
Chicago Blues
New York Nights

In the Josh Katzen Series
Hanukkah Gelt (Short)
The Pecan Pie Affair (Short)
The Case of the Moche Rolex*

In the Sitehuti and Nefer-Djenou Bastet series
To Be a Scribe (Short)
The Scribe Vanishes (Short)
Wanting the Fish (Short)
3 Tales of the Cat (Collection)s

* Coming Soon

Winter Wonderland

T. Lee Harris

Per Bastet

Winter Wonderland

Copyright © 2014 T. Lee Harris

Published by Per Bastet LLC, P.O. Box 3023 Corydon, IN 47112

Cover art by T. Lee Harris

Second Edition

ISBN 978-0-9899711-9-5

Winter Wonderland

One

It was damned cold. I had no idea just how cold that was. The electric company's digital roadside thermometer was on the fritz, as usual, and the electronic boards spanning the highway blinked between time and road information. The current temperature field was dark which told me something in itself. The software that pushed the boards had a funky little bug in it that made it blow the whole shebang if the mercury dipped below zero degrees Celsius. That was OK. I didn't really want to know. Damned cold worked — which was more than could be said for my car's heater. The heater core crapped out the day before, so I was tooling toward Louisville wearing the mega-layered look with windows down to keep the windshield from fogging up. I couldn't wait to cross the river. The nice, *windy* river.

Memories of my warm bed tried to seduce me into turning around, but I didn't have that option. I was the head of the Louisville branch of

Trueblood Investigation and Security and it was the second Wednesday of the month. That meant the regular meeting with the regional manager. The guy's name was O'Malley, he was a dead ringer for Joseph Stalin and he didn't like me much. The feeling was mutual, but that was too bad. Twenty plus years with the FBI gave me lots of practice fielding bureaucratic wonks. Having a group of home-grown terrorists drop a building on me taught me that there are worse things than being scowled at.

Most mornings, I'm the first into the office and this one was no different. I flipped on the lights, spun the thermostat off night heat and made a beeline for the closet that had delusions of kitchenhood. The pseudo-kitchen had two things to recommend it: the coffee maker and the louvered alcove where the furnace lived. I kicked the louvers open and started a pot of Kona blend.

The telephone rang just as the first fragrant stream of coffee hit the carafe. I debated answering it. Hot coffee versus cold responsibility. Hard call. Turned out I didn't have to. My receptionist, Wanda Aiken showed up like the cavalry in a puffy pink coat.

"I got it, Dallas!" she sang out.

Suited me. Coffee was kicking the crap out of responsibility and there was finally enough in the carafe for a mugful. I poured it off and drank deep. It was strong and almost too hot, but that suited me, too. I backed up against the heating vent and let the warmth from inside and out defrost me as I listened to the murmur of Wanda's telephone voice. Before long she peeked at me around the door facing. She was wearing her "oooooo I don't want to tell you this" look. Instead of telling me, she jammed a little yellow call slip in my hand and high-tailed it back to her desk. I looked at the name she'd scribbled at the top and understood. Lt. Ray Levitz of the Louisville police department, homicide division, wanted me to meet him over at the Burgess Insurance Tower construction site ASAP.

I groaned, topped off my elixir of warmth and leaned around the door. "Did you tell him about O'Malley?"

She looked up from carefully threading a hanger into her coat. "Mmmmmm, yeah. But . . . ummmm . . . he said to get your . . . ummmmm . . . backside over there, anyway."

I cleared my throat to kill a laugh. Levitz damn well didn't say backside, but Wanda just couldn't bring herself to say the word ass. Wanda belonged in another century.

Wanda also couldn't deal with the answering machine, call waiting, the fax machine or the built-in scanner. Why she was comfortable with the computer was anyone's guess. Maybe it had something to do with the fact that she liked Solitaire. Slow as business had been, she'd gotten in a lot of Solitaire practice.

I was still pondering this when my assistant, Sandy Beech, blew in. Yes, that really is his name. I've never met his parents, but they must be truly warped; he has two sisters named Virginia and Myrtle. Sandy stomped and puffed in an effort to warm up. It was surprising he was even chilled given the long woolen coat and python-length knitted scarf he wore. With his frizzy hair, he could have passed for Doctor Who. One look at his face told me he had bad news.

"Sorry, Dallas," Sandy said, unwinding the scarf. "I've been trying to reach my uncle Larry about repairing your car, but he's still at that NASCAR thing in Alabama."

Yep. It was bad. Sandy's uncle was a wizard with cars. In olden times, he'd have been burned at the stake. "Oh man," I said. "I was really hoping he could hocus-pocus the heater."

"I talked to Aunt Jay just a few minutes

ago. She thinks he'll be back tonight, but there's no way to be sure with Larry." He pointed at the coffee cup in my hands. "Is there more of that?"

I shrugged toward the kitchenette. He tossed his scarf in the general vicinity of the coat rack and bolted past me. I followed. We'd need another pot before long. I said, "Damn! Any hope for a heat wave before nightfall?"

"'Fraid not." He stirred another heaped spoonful of sugar into his coffee. Sandy didn't so much like sweetened coffee as coffee-flavored syrup. How he stayed rail-thin was beyond my comprehension. "The Ohio River Valley is notorious for wild weather swings, but not that wild. You really ought to let me play chauffeur until Larry can get your heater fixed. It's not healthy driving in this weather without it."

"Then neither of us would get anything done. Thanks for the offer, but I'll call around to find a cheap rental today — if O'Malley permits it."

"O'Malley?" Sandy shot me a deer-in-the-headlights look over the rim of his mug. "Geez, I forgot it was O'Malley Day."

"It gets better. Look at this."

Sandy took the call slip. "All this and Levitz, too. What's he want *this* time?"

"No clue, but I guess I'll find out when I get over there."

"Hey! You're already juggling fireballs, why don't I head over and. . . ?"

"Uh uh! You skated out of here and disappeared last month. No way are you going to pull that on me again." I snatched the message back, drained my mug and plunked it onto the counter. "Especially since you'll have to mind the office while I go down to find out what Levitz wants. The O'Malley mantra is that we'd have more business if I followed up a few more leads."

Sandy trailed me out into the office. "You can't do this to me, Dallas!"

Without another word, I grabbed my coat and ran for it. My plan was to head down the stairs in case O'Malley was coming up the elevator. He wasn't. He was stepping out of the elevator as I entered the hall.

"Powell! You aren't leaving, are you?"

Damn. I assumed my professional face and held out the little yellow slip "'Fraid so, O'Malley. Wanda just gave me message from Lt. Ray Levitz of LPD homicide. He wants me down at a crime scene."

He took the slip, read it and his bushy eyebrows shot up. "Is this a job?"

"I don't know, yet. I haven't talked to him."

"If it is, this could be good for the agency. Developing a liaison with the local police would be a big plus."

Liaison with the local police? Yeah, right. The TISI Louisville office had been open less than a year and, while the LPD hadn't been openly hostile to us, relations had been on the cool side. Especially with Ray Levitz and the homicide division. What I was thinking must have read on my face, because O'Malley shoved the message back into my hand and snapped: "Don't just stand there, GO!"

I went.

Two

People think of bones as gleaming white like those boiled-clean jobs you see in science labs. All well-ordered and sterile. The reality is a lot different. Hard experience hammered that into me and these hollow café au lait orbits staring up at me from the cold Kentucky clay were no exception. Café au lait was an ironic description, too. The only information Levitz had given up since I'd arrived was that the remains were found under the cellar floor of what was once a coffee shop. At least that's what the sign on the window said: Hammonds' House of Joe. The space was never rented out again and, until the day demolition began, that sign with it's over-sized coffee cup remained.

Long-time residents claimed that coffee was only *one* import available in that place — and the only legal one. Even I'd heard of it, though I'd never set foot in it. The place closed in the mid-Nineties, long before I came to Louisville. Its reputation survived the business in local legend, though, same as the over-sized coffee cup became a landmark. From the grisly memento emerging from the construction crater for the new high rise, seemed like it would survive the building, too.

"You gonna stare at her all day, or you gonna tell me what you think?"

I wrenched my gaze away from the empty sockets and turned to the cop at my side. "What I think, Levitz, is I want to know why you wanted me down here."

"Thought this would be right up your alley, what with all that Fed training an' all."

"I'm not with the Bureau anymore, remember?"

Levitz only response was to hunch farther into his coat against a gust of cold wind. I turned and walked up the side of the excavation, leaving the forensic anthropologists and photographers to their job. At the top I leaned against the seven-foot chain link construction barrier and let the cold air clear the lingering smell of decomposition from my sinuses. It helped. A little.

After a moment, Levitz followed, sounding like a wounded buffalo coming up the embankment. If a buffalo could swear, that is. Once on the sidewalk, he glowered into the slate-gray sky then bellowed into the crater, "You guys better haul ass, looks like it's gonna cut loose with snow any minute."

He smacked my sleeve as he plodded past me and on across the blocked street. "I'm a two-hundred-pound copsicle. C'mon, let's get a cappuccino or somethin' in that sandwich place over there. It's pretty good."

Inside, the shop was warm and smelled of fresh coffee and hot pastry. Nice, but it didn't help against the block of ice inside me. Remains like the ones in the construction site were part of the reason I left the Bureau. It was hard to take anonymous cases like this. Harder if you knew their names. I still wake up screaming sometimes.

I got back to business. OK, maybe a little harsher than absolutely necessary. Anyway, I said, "Dammit, Levitz, you still haven't told me why you dragged me out here. Unless I'm a suspect — farfetched considering how long those bones must have been there."

He lifted spread hands in surrender. "Slow down, Powell. Man, this got the Rompin' Heebie Jeebies going full blast, didn't it?" My head snapped around and he waved me down. "Don't give me that look. Of course I know about what happened in Montana. I may only a Louisville city cop, but I got friends in the Bureau and I like to know who I'm dealin' with. Saint Dallas Powell of the hard head and soft heart. Now shuddup an' siddown, you're makin' a scene."

I narrowed my eyes at Ray Levitz. He had the bumpkin act down so pat it was easy to underestimate him. Probably on purpose. No one ever made homicide detective by being an idiot.

Abruptly, he slid behind a table that commanded a clear view of the gate to the construction site, grabbed a laminated menu and announced, "They got a turkey soup and sandwich combo here that's deadly at thirty paces."

OK. Changing subjects was fine by me. I slid into the opposite seat. "Sounds good, you buying?"

He flashed a grin over the top of the menu, then turned toward the counter, pointed at the "Today's Specials" board and held up two fingers. Guess he was.

Turning back to me, he said, "Blame the Burgess Insurance Corporation for you bein' here. When they found out the site for their brand spankin' new corporate headquarters just become a crime scene, they went batshit. Started demandin' an independent observer to make sure the delay didn't put construction too far behind schedule. Right away, I thought of you. Your background and experience make you a shoo-in." He paused and treated me to a saccharine smile. "Unless

Trueblood Investigation and Security, Inc.'s tight-packed schedule won't permit it?"

I glared. Obviously, he knew Trueblood hadn't had so much as a divorce case in three weeks. If he knew that, he most likely also knew O'Malley was breathing down my neck. Good thing the waitress brought the food just then or I might've gone a little batshit myself. Waiting for the server to do her thing, then swish her way back to the kitchen gave me time to cool my response to: "If you're finished demonstrating your investigative prowess, maybe you'd like to tell me what we're working with. You referred to the remains as 'her' earlier?"

Levitz nodded and mumbled around a mouthful of sandwich, "Aside from the shreds of one of those fancy corset-things the lab guys already bagged and tagged, the Coroner gave me a quick take. Female, mid-twenties to mid-thirties. No readily apparent cause of death, but that'll change soon as they get her completely dug out. The demolition guys found the body when they were breakin' up the cement floor of the old coffeehouse. Lucky they was using jackhammers. If it hadda been bulldozers, there probably wouldn't be much crime scene left. Been in the ground at least ten years — I'm bettin' more like a hundred, myself. Time frame would fit with when the buildin' went up. Get a load of the pretty that was pinned to the corset." With that, he tossed me a Blackberry with a photo on the screen.

I thumbed through the pictures while I sampled the soup. The soup was as good as advertised but the photos showed both a close-up of a dirt-encrusted Victorian-looking brooch and that Levitz wasn't as all-knowing as he liked to appear. I slid the phone back across the table and said, "1928."

Levitz choked and clapped a hand over his mouth to catch a spray of masticated sourdough. He swallowed hard and rasped, "Jee-zuz, Powell. You know the date of death just by looking at a *pin*? What kind of voodoo do they teach you guys at Quantico?"

It was my turn to smile. "Not the DoD, she hasn't been dead near that long. 1928 is the name of the company that made the brooch."

My FBI training had nothing to do with the knowledge, either. Once upon a time, I'd dated a jewelry buyer for a chain of department stores and learned more about fashion trends in jewelry than I ever wanted to. The astonishment on Levitz' face almost made that three-month rollercoaster ride worthwhile. Almost.

Three

So, it looked like TISI had a job, after all. I excused myself and called Dan Ellington of Burgess Insurance to accept the job before we even finished lunch. I admit it. The fact our new client wanted me on site for as long as the crime scene was being processed made it attractive for O'Malley avoidance. The size of the fee Burgess was promising guaranteed the Lord High Bean Counter wouldn't make too big a fuss. Still, it was going to be a hard slog for me. I'd come a long way since the incidents that made me leave the Bureau. Come to grips with my inner demons, you might say, but when we returned to where the forensic team was excavating the crushed and haphazard skeleton. . . . Well, it brought back a lot of unpleasant memories.

What Levitz referred to as the "Rompin' Heebie Jeebies," was officially called Post Traumatic Stress Disorder. A nice way to say what I'd been through freaked me out. Big time. Being buried alive in rubble that used to be a federal office building can do that to a person. There was more to it than that, though.

Before the bad guys blew up the regional FBI office with me and my colleagues in it, we'd been investigating the murder of three fellow agents — friends — by a group of white supremacists. When we finally found their graves, there was a little more left of them than of this nameless victim. A little. But not much.

My phone cheeped, announcing a text message. It was from Sandy, a veiled threat against my well-being for abandoning him with O'Mally and a reminder that we needed more coffee. I sent a suitably snarky reply and pocketed the phone with a chuckle. The intrusion of the everyday helped. I took a deep breath, jammed my hands in my pockets and managed to focus attention on what was going on in front of me, which was not much.

The forensic team wasn't making much progress and Levitz was pacing and growling like a caged bear. Ray's weather prediction had proved true and snow sifted down in a fine white mist. The team had erected a shelter before the snow began and brought in lights to augment the gray winter daylight, but the surrounding ground was quickly turning white and the wind drifted the powder into the excavation. The Coroner wasn't a woman given to profanity, but there were occasional eruptions of "Oh sugar!" or "Fudge!" rising from the hole. I admired her restraint, it was a less than optimal situation. When she and her team finally finished a little after six p.m., my immediate need to document anything for my new client was finished, too. Once the remains hit the morgue, I knew there wouldn't be a big hurry to get to them. With a case this old and a fully skeletonized body, there rarely is.

As I stood there watching the techs break down the lights and tent in the falling snow, I realized I wasn't in much of a hurry, either. What? Rush back into the jaws of the Lord High Bean Counter? Not on your life. I'd burned up enough air time with him as it was. Between O'Malley and Dan Ellington they'd almost drained my phone battery. That didn't even touch on Sandy's running text commentary. No. What I really wanted to do was crawl into a hole and pull myself back together. That didn't rank high on the probability charts, though.

Looking at the low battery icon, I wondered if I had enough juice to call a cab to cart me back to the office. My thumb hovered over the redial button for the same company that had hauled me to the site earlier, then changed my mind. It was only a few blocks to the office. I was cold already. Why not walk? Especially since the Jade Dragon oriental restaurant was conveniently located between here and there. Closer to here than there. Sounded good: a warm place to sit down, friendly people to talk to and the prospect of something other than a microwaved frozen dinner, to boot. I dropped the phone in my pocket shut and slogged off.

The aromas seeping out of the Jade Dragon started working on me before I could even see the sign over the door. That was going some. The sign was a neon masterpiece depicting a twisting Chinese dragon in vivid red, blue and green. Tonight, the neon beacon painted splashes of color over the collecting snow as I urged frozen muscles toward the good smells.

Inside, the place was packed with dragons, most of them plastic, except for the one in the glass case behind the cash register. That was one venerable worm. Genuine white jade, a family treasure for better than 600 years, and the piece itself was thought to be much older than that. According to Harvey Leong, Prop., it was a sky dragon. Didn't mean much to me, but beaucoup to Harve. Once I asked why the thing wasn't in a bank vault or on loan to a nice, safe museum and was told the dragon had to preside over the family doings. It was tradition. Tradition maybe, but lousy security. I guess the best protection was that no one believed anything so valuable would be on such prominent display in a hole-in-the-wall eatery like the one bearing its name.

Still, the dragon's magic seemed to be working. The place was also packed with people. I gave the kid working the counter my carry-out order and wandered into the dining area to wait without much hope my usual booth would be open. To my surprise, it was. First good news I'd had all day. I slid onto the worn vinyl seat, sat back, and let the central heating work on me. I was just warmed enough to shuck my coat when a bottle of Ki-Rin beer plunked onto the table and Harve Leong, plunked into the opposite seat.

"Looks like you need this," he twanged.

It was weird hearing a Kentucky drawl coming out of a guy who looked like supporting cast for *The Last Son of Heaven*, but that was Harve right down to the ground. He was third generation Louisvillian on account of his great grandparents followed the railroads from the west coast as far as Louisville, then settled in. They swore blue that it was because the Ohio River valley looked like a great place to raise a family. Pam Leong, always the cynic, suspected it was simply where the money ran out. Pam's childhood in Vietnam left her with a lot of doubts about human nature. Coming home with a gem of a GI husband like Harve only went a little way to smooth those over.

"Right the first time, Harve." I took a sip of the beer, then gestured at the dining area. "Looks like things are going good for you, though."

He took in the crowd and nodded. "Can't complain. You look like you been dragged three miles over a gravel road, though. Wanna talk about it?"

"O'Malley Day."

He took a long and considered pull on his own bottle of beer. "That all? You look like y'seen a ghost."

Harve is a little older than me. He was in Viet Nam during some of the worst fighting and came home with Post Traumatic Stress Disorder before they even had a name for it. When he found out who I was and what had happened . . . well, I found I could talk to Harve. "Guess maybe I did. I've been working a crime scene all day with Ray Levitz from LPD."

Harve nodded. "Oh."

About then a big plate of steaming Crab Rangoon slid onto the table as suddenly as the beer had appeared. I looked up to find Pam Leong frowning at us. Harve came home from Vietnam with more than just PTSD. He also brought home a doll of a Vietnamese wife. She jabbed a finger at him. "You! What you trying to do giving beer to man with empty stomach. Sometimes you just got no sense." So I didn't feel left out, she wheeled on me, too. "You just as bad! Run around in snow. Make yourself sick. Eat!"

She marched back into the kitchen muttering in Vietnamese. I was real glad I didn't understand a word of it. Harve chuckled. "Jimmy squealed on you when he brought your order back. Said you came in lookin' like a Yeti. Car still down?"

"Yeah, and Sandy let me know about an hour ago, his uncle is at some kind of NASCAR thing until the end of the week. It isn't likely to back up soon."

"Not good. Tell you what, I got a nephew who's gettin' into cars. Lemme see what he can come up with."

Knowing most of Harve's nephews, I was dubious. I was also desperate. "Sure. Anything as long as it has a heater!" I'd come to regret those words.

Harve and I munched and shot the breeze for a while before my order came. I think Pam dragged her feet to allow me decompression time. It worked. By the time I hopped in a cab back to the office, I felt much better. The fact I hadn't had a call from O'Malley for more than an hour didn't hurt either.

The cab dropped me off in the parking lot of my building. I was a little unhappy to see O'Malley's car was still there and all the lights in the office were on. I considered going up, but decided against it. If O'Malley had any more questions, he would have called, right? Sure! He hadn't been shy about it before. I unlocked my car. No sooner had I reached across to put my bag of dinner on the passenger seat when my cell rang. O'Malley.

"Powell, you weren't going home without checking in, were you?"

"Of course not. I was just on my way up, I had to put some stuff in the car first."

"Good. I have a few questions about the receipts for the Hudson case."

"Be right there."

I made sure not to slam the door too hard or kick anything on the way in since the Lord High Bean Counter was watching. Wouldn't give him the satisfaction. He was probably rubbing his hands together in anticipation of making me explain something like twenty-two admissions to Six Flags Over Kentucky and forty-eight corn dogs. Hey. That's what happens when your witness is a Boy Scout troop.

Four

Much, much later, I turned off of the main road, drove between two creek rock light standards and right into another time. The walls of trimmed box elder and heavy canopy of trees blocked the noises from the busy street outside, and the big snow-covered Victorian houses looked like Christmas card paintings. It could have been a set for an Andy Hardy movie.

I was an Army brat. My Dad's career took us all over the country and all over the globe. Don't get me wrong, we lived in some great places. Still, all of those places had one thing in common: they weren't home.

Even after I joined the Bureau, I was a nomad. Throughout my career, I'd been offered and accepted posts all over and lived in a steady stream of apartments, condos, rentals — all nice places. Still none of them were home. Truth to tell, I'm not sure I knew what home was or even that I was looking for it until I moved to the Louisville area and the rental agent gave me Mrs. Overholzer's address. It sounds corny, I know, but I knew I wanted to live here even before I saw the converted upstairs of Mrs. Overholzer's house.

I continued down to the last house on the left, pulled in the drive and onto the parking slab in back of my apartment, shut off the engine and picked up the bag with my dinner cartons. They crunched. Looked like microwaved frozen food tonight, anyway.

At the foot of the back stairs, my landlady came out and hailed me. She was wearing her stern look and holding my cat, Hoover. Well, I say that, but Hoover isn't really my cat. He sorta came with the apartment. He's either a gray Persian mix or a long-haired gray tabby who's been chasing parked cars and caught one.

I braced myself. "What's he done this time, Mrs. O?"

She thrust the cat at me and I juggled the carry-out bag to take him. "Your cat was terrorizing my poor little Beau again."

Contrary to appearances, my landlady actually likes me. Normally we had a good relationship, but it was in the crapper when Beau and Hoover mixed it up — which was whenever Beau got out.

"Poor little Beau" was a Yorkie, and I'd have to say the most foul-tempered one I'd seen. Not the brightest bulb in the canine chandelier, either. He never seemed to catch on that Hoover was twice his size. All he saw was "cat" and so picked a fight every time he could with predictable results. Predictable to everyone but Beau.

"Sorry Mrs. O."

"Mr. Powell, you simply must control your cat! Responsibility is the key to pet ownership."

I started to remind her that he wasn't my cat, but stopped myself. Been there, said that, nobody listens. Especially the cat. Besides, Mrs. O was already back in the house. Hoover squirmed out of my grasp, trotted up the steps and disappeared through the cat door I'd installed when I got tired of him waking me up at all hours to go out. Considering how drastically the temperature had dipped after sunset, he had the right idea. I followed him up hoping that at least the microwave still worked.

Inside, I stepped around Hoover, punched "Play" on the stereo and headed for the kitchen. Chet Baker's trumpet flooded the living room as I pulled metal bails off food cartons and piled them into the microwave. It was only then that I shucked my coat and dropped my cell into the docking station. O'Malley, Sandy and Dan Ellington gave it had a workout earlier and I fully expected it would get another tonight. It was one of Mom's regular nights to call and the last thing I wanted was for the battery to cut out while I was talking to her. Days like today made me question the decision to have only a cell phone, but days like today were few and far enough between, so I let it ride.

The food had several minutes to go, ample time to get on line and check e-mail. Sandy'd been stuck with the Lord High Bean Counter all day, so I anticipated several outrageous messages. I was not disappointed. Along with the ubiquitous mountain of spam, there were seven from Sandy, including an e-card promising revenge and one message from my sister with the subject of "Mom Alert." It was tempting fate — or at least tempting Mom calling before I read the message, but I couldn't face it on an empty stomach. I deleted the spam and entertained myself with Sandy's messages until the microwave beeped. I glopped General Tso's Chicken into the top of the fried rice carton, grabbed a plastic fork, then returned to Sandy's e-mail. Was I being a coward? Hell yeah!

I already knew what the message was about, anyway. Well, not *exactly* what it was about, just close enough. It started right after I was released from the hospital where I'd spent about a year undergoing physical therapy and learning to walk again. The chunk of building that pinned my legs after the bombing did massive damage to more than my body. It got my Mom's already active worry glands pumping into overdrive. That got worse after 9/11. My father, who is a full bird Army colonel, works at the Pentagon. Dad was on the opposite side of the building when the plane hit, but it was too close for Mom. Convinced that fate was out to ace the whole family, she started finding "wonderful jobs" for my sister and me right there in the DC area. We could all be together, wasn't that lovely?

I have refrained from commenting that if the family were all in one place, it would be easier for the Big Bads to take us all out in one Big Bang. Mom was never strong in the humor department. She's even less so now.

My sister Trish is an advertising executive in San Francisco. I suspect she chose San Francisco because that was almost as far away from DC as she could get without leaving the country. She also has applied for positions in both Alaska and Hawaii. More than likely, she's still trying. It isn't that we hate our parents or anything like that, it's just that Mom tends to be overprotective and Dad tends to be overcontrolling.

When I finally opened Trish's e-mail, it was what I expected. Mom had talked to this guy who was high up in the NSA and they'd just love for me to come work there. She was counting on Trish to back her up and help convince me. It would be an incredible opportunity and they couldn't let me turn away from it . . . etcetera, etcetera, etcetera. For once, my timing was good. Mom called just as I sent my reply to Trish. Thank God for free family calls after five, because we "discussed" my future until almost midnight.

Five

The phone woke me a half-hour before my alarm was set to go off. I fumbled it into the general vicinity of my face. "Mmmmph . . . Powell. . . ."

Harve Leong guffawed into the phone. "Geez, musta been a real wild one last night!"

"Yeah, a laugh a minute. What is it, Harve?"

"Remember I told you about my nephew, Clarence, gettin' into cars?"

That worked better than coffee. I swung my legs over the edge of the bed. "Yeah, I remember. He has one I can use?"

"Sure does, now trot that half-dead Honda of yours over to the shop. Clarence says he'll have the loaner over to your office at the Heyburn Building before noon."

I stumbled into the kitchen and punched the brew button on the coffee maker. "Any idea what he's got?"

"Nope. All I know is Clarence says it runs great and has a heater that'll run you right outta the car."

"Sounds good. Thanks, Harve!"

I'd called ahead, but the guys at the auto shop still weren't real enthusiastic about me bringing the car in that morning. They got happier when I told them I had a loaner lined up and there wasn't a big hurry getting it back. Can't complain, though. Once I got there, they wouldn't let me call a cab, but insisted that one of the mechanics give me a lift to the office. Aside from getting a dissertation on the inner secrets of heater cores, it was a pleasant drive.

That was good because things got back to normal fast. I barely made it through the door before Wanda thrust a handful of call slips at me along with a cup of coffee. I sipped the coffee and read the slips. All but one were calls from Dan Ellington of Burgess Insurance. The other one was from O'Malley wanting an update on the Burgess job.

She asked, "You want me to get Mr. Ellington on the phone for you?"

Bless the woman. She didn't even consider asking if I wanted to talk to O'Malley. I shook my head. "Not yet, see if you can get Levitz first."

Unfortunately, the Powell Luck was back in full force. Before I could finish the sentence, the phone rang. Ellington. I sighed and took the receiver Wanda held out to me. It was not a good conversation. As the guy who was signing the check, Ellington wanted to know more on the status of the case. Very understandable. Unfortunately, I couldn't give him what I didn't have myself.

It was even more unfortunate that wasn't about to change soon. Wanda put in calls for Levitz several times before lunch and got the same answer each time: "He just stepped out." This was a pattern I would come to know and loathe.

The closer the clock edged toward noon, the antsier I got about Harve's nephew, too. None of the Leong clan was noted for punctuality, but telling myself that didn't help. I was fingering my cell phone when Clarence finally poked his head into my office and tossed me a set of car keys. "Betcha thought I wasn't goin' to make it, huh?"

"It had crossed my mind."

"Hey, better late than never. C'mon, I parked so we can see it from your office window."

Fairly bursting with pride, he pulled me over to the window and pointed to the parking spaces below. I scanned the lot for an unfamiliar vehicle, but all I could see was something that looked like a silver and rust polka-dot egg. No. Hell no. "Uh,

Clarence. What is that?"

"It's a '76 Pacer. Ain't she a beauty?"

"She's . . . something."

Clarence glowed. "The guy I got it from was actually asking six hundred for it, but he came down to four hundred easy. Can you believe it? Four hundred for a classic like that?"

I was glad he didn't need a response from me, because all I could do was stare at the thing. An egg. A polka-dot egg. Glad it was only temporary.

Six

When my apartment doorbell rang one evening later that week, I thought it was the delivery kid from the Pizza King down the street. Instead it was Levitz with a thick manila envelope under his arm. I was proud of my restraint as I said, "Levitz, you sonuvabitch! You've been ducking me."

Levitz laughed. "Good to see you, too, Powell. Nice digs, ya gonna ask me to sit down or just snarl at me from the doorway?"

"I might ask you to take a header off the fire escape. You set me up, Levitz, you told Dan Ellington I was your choice for the company's police liaison then you leave me flapping in the wind with no information and Ellington calling me at least twice a day for the last four days."

"Shoulda come down to the station."

"I did. You 'just stepped out' — all day long. Four days in a row."

Levitz flumphed onto the couch without

invitation. "Musta been Sergeant Searcy, he never knows what's goin' on." He jerked a thumb over his shoulder. "Hey, what's that polka dot thing down on the parking pad?"

"A Pacer. It's a classic."

"No shit? What happened to the Honda?"

Levitz must have a guardian angel because the kid with the pizza came through the still-open door behind me. "Twenny-one sixty, Mr. Powell." He looked down at the floor and grinned. "Hey, Hoover, how's it goin'?"

I snarled at the cat. "Where the hell have you been all day? It's an epidemic. Ignore Dallas, then show up on his doorstep when dinner comes."

Yep, he ignored me and continued to make nice with the delivery guy. After all, he was the guy with the food. I fished out a twenty and a five and handed it to the kid, who stuffed it into his cash bag and disappeared down the stairs with: "Thanks Mr. Powell!" He could have at least waited for me to tell him to keep the change.

I kicked the door closed and got out the paper plates. OK, I hate doing dishes. Sue me. "You better be here for more than mooching food, Ray."

"Powell, I'm wounded." He held the over-stuffed manila envelope up. "You'd begrudge a smidge of pizza to the bearer of an eye-popping forensics report?"

Smidge. In his whole life, Levitz never settled for a smidge of anything. Ignoring him, I poured kitty kibble into Hoover's bowl then added a hunk of cheese and sausage from the pizza. Hoover jammed his face into it before it even reached the floor.

"Powell, you're a loon," Levitz said. "You name your cat after J. Edgar and you feed him pizza?"

"He didn't get his name because he looked like J. Edgar — although he does. It's mostly because of the way he vacuums up food," I said. I plunked the pizza box, paper plates and a roll of paper towels on the coffee table. "And you better believe I share the pizza with him. It's a lot easier than battling him for every bite I take. Think of it as paying protection."

Levitz watched the cat who had his face buried to the ears in the food bowl and nodded. We munched in silence for a couple minutes. When the edge was off my hunger, I motioned toward the envelope and said, "OK, you've had your smidge, now pop my eyes."

Levitz looked smug. "Bet I can surprise you this time. It's a guy."

He was right. I was surprised. "But the Coroner said. . . ."

"That was before they got her — *him* dug out. Once the Coroner saw the pelvis completely free of dirt at the lab, she about had a fit. Said something about being fooled by the lacies and a gracile bone structure. That changed our ID search criteria a little."

"Good thing the skeleton was complete. You could have been spinning your wheels in the wrong direction for a long time. Got a name yet?"

"Yeah. That's where *I* get a surprise. Our vic is none other than Jess Wynan."

"You say that like I should recognize the name."

"I keep forgetting you're not from around here. The Wynans been in building for almost as long as Louisville's been here. Jess' daddy built the business into one of the biggest contracting concerns around. In the early seventies, Daddy keeled over on the back nine with a coronary. Left Jess a bundle along with control of the family business."

"Let me guess," I said around a mouthful of pizza. "Jess wanted to be more than just a contractor."

"You got it," said Levitz, "Started throwing money around. Political campaigns, charities — the usual high profile stuff. Anyways, when the

Bi-Centennial celebration got closer, a lot of cities got heavy into. . . ," he wiped grease off his fingers, dropped the stained paper towel onto the pile next to his plate and fished a sheaf of papers from the envelope. "Yeah. Restoration and Beautification Projects is what it was called."

I nodded. "I remember that. Towns all across the country got into that act."

"Yep. So did Jess Wynan and Wynan Construction, Inc. He spearheaded a foundation to award grants to small business owners to renovate the downtown area for the Bicentennial doings. That's where we have our connection with the Hammonds."

"Ah, now this name I know. Weren't they the owners of the block Burgess bought and the coffeehouse in particular? It was Hammond's House of Joe?"

"Bingo. Sherm and Delia Hammond. Real savory characters and a marriage made in hell. Around the mid-seventies, Sherm and Delia decided to clean up their act — sorta. They jumped into the renovation shindig same time as Jess. It was a Wynan grant helped them give the old pile a face-lift right around the time Jess disappeared.

"We also got a cause of death, too." He peeled a few pages from the sheaf and slid them across the table at me. The Coroner's report. Levitz jabbed a finger at the COD line. "Several powerful blows to the back of the head with a hammer. Looks like the killer was real P.O.ed at ol' Jess. One whack woulda done the job, but the Coroner figures more like five. Plus, there's both blond and brown hairs caught in the wound as well as nylon mesh fibers. The brown hairs match the hair found in the grave and Jess' physical description; we figger he was wearin' a wig when he got clobbered. Fits with the lacy long-johns."

"It all fits. Why do I think you don't like this?"

"I dunno. Maybe because this guy never struck me as the queer type. I mean, he was one of the biggest playboys in town. Always had a pretty woman on his arm. Hard to think of this guy prancing around in a wig and corset."

I smirked. "Hey, they claim J. Edgar, himself, went in drag."

It was Levitz' turn to glare. He opened his mouth to retort, but instead bellowed and dived for the floor. I was startled until Hoover (the cat, not the other guy) shot from under the coffee table and vanished out the cat door with Levitz' last piece of pizza in his teeth.

Seven

Turns out what Levitz dropped by for was so I could go with him to interview Delia Hammond. Seems Sherm was ten years dead and Delia didn't look to be far behind. She was a patient the Whispering Oaks Convalescent Home in the terminal stages of emphysema. Levitz didn't want to waste any time.

I'd heard Whispering Oaks was an upscale place, but that didn't half cover it. It was a sprawling stone pile surrounded by a couple acres of manicured grounds all wrapped up in an eight-foot-high brick wall. The public entrance was through a set of big iron gates they must've bought off a bankrupt English manor. There was probably a separate entrance for staff and other low-life like cops and PIs, but Levitz pulled his battered, unmarked sedan up to the main gate. It was closed, but there was one of those little intercom/closed circuit TV units set into the wall on the driver's side. Levitz punched the button and held his shield and ID up to the tiny camera. "Lt. Ray Levitz from Louisville Metro Police Department. You got somebody in charge out here?"

The lobby must have come from the same English manor with dark oak paneling and a huge crystal chandelier. A severe-looking woman in a no-frills beige linen suit met us under it. From her expression, I gathered she'd like to have dropped the thing on us and be done with it. She said, "I'm Mrs. Le Coeur, the nursing supervisor. How may I help you?"

Levitz flipped his ID case open again. "I'm Lt. Ray Levitz of Louisville Police and this is Mr. Dallas Powell representing the Burgess Insurance Corporation. We'd like to speak with a patient of yours, Mrs. Delia Hammond."

Neither ID nor introduction made a dent. "Visiting hours are from eight a.m. to seven p.m."

"I'm aware of that ma'am, but we need to speak to Mrs. Hammond now — it's police business."

She relented and ordered us to come to her office. I felt like a ten-year-old caught with a *Playboy* magazine in school. The impression was heightened when she sat behind a desk the size of a helipad and lifted the telephone. "Mrs. Hammond is under private care, you'll have to speak with her nurse, Ms. Soward. I'll have her here in a minute."

Levitz was undeterred. "Thanks for the offer, Mrs. Le Coeur, but I think we'd rather talk in private if you don't mind."

She minded, but she took us to a visitor area anyway. Looking around the room, I wondered if they'd simply bought a whole manor house and reconstructed it stone by stone in Louisville. I lowered myself into a chair that was probably worth more than my car and asked, "So what was wrong with Mrs. Le Coeur's office?"

Levitz looked at me like I'd sprouted a tail. "You really think the Grand Pooh-Bah would vacate to let us talk to the nurse by our lonesome? Nu uh. I know the type. She'd at least have had her ear glued to the intercom pickup." He stomped around examining the walls, stopped in front of a huge floral spray and said, "If there's an intercom in this room, I can't find it. Old biddy sure was P.O.ed, wasn't she? Never trust anyone like that in a room with an intercom." He took in the rest of the room and spat, "Crime don't pay, huh? Couldn't prove it by me. Damn. My Mammaw was a saint if there ever was one and the place she spent her final years in wasn't as nice as this place's mop closet."

He broke off as a beautiful brunette in a nurse's uniform stepped through the door. Her eyes flicked nervously between us. "Are you the policemen who want to see Mrs. Hammond?"

I smiled and jerked a thumb at Levitz. "He is, I'm Dallas Powell, a Private Investigator representing the Burgess Insurance Corporation. You're Ms. Soward?"

"Phyllis Soward." Her handshake was firm and dry. She smiled ruefully. "I'm sorry, gentlemen, you're going to like this, but I can't let you in to see Mrs. Hammond."

Scowling, Levitz stepped forward with the ubiquitous ID held up at eye level. "Lt. Ray Levitz. Homicide. May I ask why not?"

Ms. Soward didn't flinch but gave the big cop a cool, steady look. "It isn't my decision. I have standing orders not to let anyone into her room without family or doctor permission."

I stepped in. "Does she have many visitors?"

"I couldn't say. I've only been tending her for a month, but in the time I've been with her, there haven't been many."

"You're new then?"

She laughed. "Very few of Mrs. Hammond's employees are old hands. She's been here ten months and I'm nurse number eight." She went quiet and indecision flashed across her face, then she glanced out in the hall before continuing. "From what I understand, Delia Hammond has never had a sunny attitude and the pain she's in doesn't help an already bad temper. She heaps abuse on anyone who comes into range. She's made a point of not remembering my name, if that tells you anything."

"Why do you stick it out?"

"I've never been a quitter, Mr. Powell. You know she's terminal?" At my nod, she continued, "I've tended terminal patients before and all the signs are there. It won't be long now." She shrugged. "I can put up with the unpleasantness for a little longer. The conditions are bad, but the paycheck is good and the signing bonus I got was sweet."

I glanced at Levitz to see if he had anything to add, but he seemed content to let me do the asking. I said, "Does Delia keep up on the news?"

Phyllis rolled her eyes. "I'll say! I have to read the paper to her every morning from front page to comics."

"Then she's heard about the skeleton they found at the Burgess construction site. Did she have a reaction to the news?"

Phyllis' eyes widened. "Why, yes! Her reaction was odd, though. She made me read parts of the story twice. Been quieter since. It was like . . . I don't know . . . kind of like the other shoe finally dropped? You know what I mean?"

"Yeah. I think I do."

Her face clouded as she clicked two and two together. "The paper said that was a murder. Is that what this is about?"

I opened my mouth to answer, but Levitz jumped in at last. "Yeah it is. Gonna let us talk to Delia now?"

She shook her head. "Look, I'm not trying to be difficult, but I have my instructions from her daughter, Jessica — *Ms*. Hammond. I can't let anyone in unless she gives the OK. You'd need to clear it with her before I can do anything. I don't ask why, I just cash the paycheck. The really *nice* paycheck. Believe you me, if it wasn't so nice, you'd be either eating my dust or talking to someone else."

Levitz looked geared to blow, but Phyllis was unfazed. She gave us another level look and said, "It's not like it would do you much good if I let you in tonight, anyway. She's already had her evening meds and the stuff they've got her on knocks her out for at least six hours." A pause. "Seven, if I'm lucky."

Levitz groused, but there wasn't much he could do short of getting a warrant and he didn't have near enough for that. I enjoyed watching Ray squirm, then grinned at Phyllis and pressed my business card into her hand. "OK, we'll talk to Ms. Hammond, but how about you slip this to *Mrs.* Hammond when she wakes up. That's not exactly letting anyone in, right?"

She took my card and the one Levitz gave her with a doubtful look. I noticed she made no promises. Instead, she pulled a small notebook and a gold pen from her pocket, wrote and ripped the page out. She handed me the paper. "This is Jessica Hammond's address and phone number. I wish you luck with her. I have as little to do with her as possible. She isn't the hellion her mother is . . . but . . . I just plain don't like her. She's dumped responsibility of her mother on me, the doctors and the staff of Whispering Oaks and makes no secret she's glad to be shed of her. I don't know, maybe if my mother was as nasty as Delia, I'd do the same."

Eight

It was late and getting later, but we headed over to Jessica Hammond's place, anyway. We didn't bother to call ahead, from the scathing looks Mrs. Le Coeur gave us as we left, we figured she'd already done the calling for us. She had. When we pulled into the driveway and got out of the car, the door to the house flew open and a woman silhouetted against the interior light called, "Who the hell are you? You're not my lawyer — if you're the cops, you can just cool your heels until my legal advisor gets here."

This was bad. I had images of Levitz and me sitting for hours in the freezing car waiting to be chewed up and spat out by ravening lawyers. I was wrong, though. Jessica Hammond was too impulsive and too fired-up to do the smart thing and slam the door on us. Instead, she tore down the front steps shouting, "How dare you disturb a dying woman at this time of night? Nothing can be that important. I'll have you know I've already

lodged a complaint with your superiors!" All this
and she hadn't even asked for ID.

Levitz went through his usual spiel, holding his
shield and card toward the wedge of light spilling
from the open front door. I admired his tenacity;
so far all this had accomplished was to open the
gate at Whispering Oaks. This time it had an
effect, but not the one he wanted. Upon hearing
my name and who I represented, she wheeled on
me. "I don't understand what problem Burgess
has that involves Mother, the sale is a done deal.
The building was mine to sell and Mother had
nothing to do with it."

Snapping his ID case closed, Levitz moved in.
"Maybe you haven't heard they found the remains
of a murder victim under the cement floor of the
building your parents owned?"

This was old news and we were boring her
already. "Of course I did. My parents used to own
that whole block — they owned a lot of property
in the Louisville area. So?"

Something wasn't clicking with her. He tried
again. "So we found somebody whose head was
bashed in buried in the basement of a building
your parents owned and ran a business out of and
we want to talk to your Mama about it."

She exhaled an exasperated humph. "Lots of

people ran businesses out of that building. I'd imagine most of them had access to the basement, why not go bother them? This doesn't have anything to do with us."

I asked, "It doesn't? What do you know about Jess Wynan?"

Jessica turned toward me so that the light from the door fell across her, revealing a delicate face at odds with the shrill voice. She looked puzzled. "Who? Oh, I remember . . . the Wynan Old Louisville Trust. My parents had some business dealings with them. He had something to do with real estate, didn't he? Oh. Was that him — I thought the papers said it was a woman's body?"

Levitz said, "It was contracting, not real estate and yes, the remains have been identified as those of Jess Wynan who has been missing since 1975."

She shrugged. "I couldn't have known him then, I wasn't born until 1976. Look, will you get to the point? I have an early day tomorrow."

I interjected, "Dan Ellington of Burgess Insurance tells us that they've been trying to buy that property for a couple years and your mother wouldn't sell. Suddenly, you took their offer. Why was that?"

For the first time Jessica looked doubtful, but

she dismissed it. "My parents ran a little coffee shop down there. It was their first business so Mother had certain sentimental attachments and didn't want to see an impersonal office building go in. My parents gifted me the properties when I reached twenty-one and they became fully mine on my twenty-fifth birthday. Nothing warm and fuzzy on my parent's part, I assure you. My father set up my trust fund before he died and my mother went along with it as a way to cheat the state out of inheritance taxes."

Her answer was very flat. Cold. I said, "And you sold it."

"They offered me a lot of money and I don't have those sentiments."

Or many others, I'd wager. Headlights from a car pulling into the drive in back of us flooded the scene with a blinding glare. The driver got out without shutting off the engine or the lights. Jessica glanced at the newcomer approaching our little group and said loudly, "I'm afraid I'm going to have to refuse you. I can't allow you to disturb a dying old woman with questions she couldn't possibly answer."

Levitz snarled, "OK. We'll just have to talk to a judge, then."

The newcomer was the tardy lawyer, who

introduced himself as Terrence Newman. He snapped, "You do that, mister. You'd better have a warrant before you come sniffing around Ms. Hammond or her mother again or I'll have your badges."

The lawyer and Levitz locked horns for a few more minutes, leaving Jessica Hammond and me on the edges of the battle. I took the opportunity to give her a once-over. She was tall, slim and expensively dressed. Her dark hair was done up in the latest style — fairly recently from the look of it. She stood in the glare of the lawyer's headlights, lit a cigarette and settled back to enjoy the fight. I noted the barely concealed glee at the fracas and found myself agreeing with Phyllis Soward's assessment of the lady. There was something else that rang wrong. Call me a cynic, but I got the feeling there was more than a professional relationship between the lady and the lawyer. Nothing I could put my finger on, but . . . something.

It was extremely late by the time I got home and fell into bed.

The phone was already ringing as I slipped the key into the office door the next morning. I fumbled the lock open and dove for it. "Trueblood Investigation and Security, Inc. Dallas Powell speaking."

There was a sigh of relief on the other end and a woman's voice came over the wire, "Thank God I finally got you, Mr. Powell. This is Phyllis Soward — we met last night at the Whispering Oaks Convalescent Center?"

"Yes, Ms. Soward, I remember. You sound rattled, has something happened?"

"I'll say it has. When Mrs. Hammond woke up this morning, I told her about your visit and gave her your cards like you asked. I thought she was having another attack. She insisted I call you right away and well, your home number wasn't on the card and you aren't in the Louisville directory. . . ."

"It wouldn't be, I only have a cell. Does Mrs. Hammond want to see me? That might be difficult, her daughter refused to let us interview her. Even sicced an attack lawyer on us."

"Terry Newman, I bet." Phyllis laughed a little in spite of everything, then caught herself. "I don't think that visiting will be a problem. Delia is causing such a fuss and refusing any medications until you get here, Mrs. Le Coeur will be overjoyed to see you. She might even carry you into the room herself."

"Let me get Lt. Levitz and we're on our way."

She thanked me and apologized again for calling so early before she hung up. I dialed Levitz and found myself hoping this case would last long enough for me to get to know Phyllis better. Sgt. Searcy picked up and I said, "This is Dallas Powell for Ray Levitz, and before you tell me he isn't available, maybe you ought to tell him I got us in to see Delia Hammond right away."

Worked like a charm. Levitz didn't bother to pick up, just had Searcy tell me to be ready to roll when he got to my doorstep.

Nine

Phyllis called it. Mrs. Le Coeur welcomed us with open relief and all but dragged us down the hall. She tapped once on the half-open door and pulled us into the sickroom.

Delia Hammond was propped up in a hospital bed surrounded with starched white pillows and sheets that accented the unhealthy yellow of her skin and eyes. Seeing her like this was a bit of a shock. The mental image I had of her was built from the photos and clippings in the files. The statuesque, shapely brunette had withered to a scarecrow with sparse colorless hair and stretched parchment skin. Only the eyes were the same, blue steel that bored a hole through each of us as we entered.

Mrs. Le Coeur said, "These are the gentlemen from the insurance company you wanted to see." Then she beat a hasty retreat. Phyllis was hard on her heels. Looking on the face of the Dragon Lady, herself, I wished I could go with them.

"I know you," Delia said pointing a shaking

finger at Levitz. "You ain't no insurance guy, you're a goddam cop!" The outburst took a lot out of her, she sagged against the pillows, scrabbled for the oxygen feed and took a long pull. When her breathing regulated, she said, "Ah, it don't matter. Place'll be lousy with cops since you found Jess. I told Sherm we shoulda dug deeper. Stupid sonuvabitch never wanted to do a lick more than he absolutely had to." She pinned Levitz with the steel glare. "I know you figured out it's Jess Wynan in that hole. My daughter was burnin' up the phone lines first thing this mornin'."

"Are you telling me that you and your husband killed Wynan?" Nonplussed, Levitz plopped into a chair. "If I'da known this was gonna be a confession, I'da brought a tape recorder."

Her laugh turned into hard coughing again. "Tough. Write it down later. You got more time than I do, so lissen up." She took a few more drags on her oxygen, then said, "When me and Sherm opened that coffee shop, we was strictly small time. Little bit o' fencing, little bit o' dealing — that sort of thing. That was back in the 70s, just when the hoohah for the Bi-Centennial was gearing up. There was all kinds of money floating around then in the shape of grants, we jumped on the bandwagon hoping to hook a little for ourselves."

Her voice trailed and she took another hit of oxygen. The steely blue eyes closed.

Levitz had pulled a beat up spiral-bound notepad and pen from his pocket when she started to talk. From my position on the other side of the bed, I could just see the page he'd started. I almost laughed out loud when I recognized the chicken scratches as shorthand. Who'da thunk it, right? The lieutenant watched her for a moment, then prompted, "That's how you and Sherm hooked up with Wynan, right."

"Hooked up. Good way to say it," Delia said without opening her eyes. "Yeah. Sherm and me met Jess through the Old Louisville Trust. His family was richer than Croesus and decided to spread it around by renovating the older parts of the city. We got a grant to pretty up the old building our store was in. Place was a dump, but had history, so we got the money and we got to know Jess. Jess knew Louisville was growin' fast and wanted to buy into the downtown district, but on the QT. Y'know, to avoid taxes and all that crap. Me and Sherm had lots of connections and was wantin' to improve our own financial situation, too. So Jess made us some private loans and we was buyin' up property around Louisville, slow-like so as not to draw a lot of attention."

"So Wynan became your silent partner?" Levitz asked.

Delia nodded faintly. "That's the way it started out. Strictly business — and we were damned good at it. Before two years passed, me and Sherm owned the building our shop was in and most of the buildings on the block, too. We were ridin' high. Everything was goin' our way."

Scarecrow fingers spasmed and the oxygen feed bounced away to dangle off the edge of the bed. I retrieved it, put it on the pillow beside her and said, "Sounds like something happened to change that."

"You got that right. Everything started out all business, but Jess never could let well enough alone. Couldn't stand for things to stay quiet too long. Got twitchy. Had to stir things up. Pretty soon he made advances t'me and I didn't say no." Steel-blue eyes slid toward me as if I'd asked a question. She snapped, "Do I look stupid? He was a real looker and all that Wynan money didn't hurt none. I wasn't so bad in them days, either. We had a great time for a while. Private dinners, weekends up in French Lick—" Another coughing fit interrupted her, leaving her wheezing, oxygen mask pressed tight to her face with both hands.

Levitz leaned forward looking grim. Finally,

he stood and said, "Look, maybe we better let you rest and take up later—"

"*No!*" It was the strongest I'd heard her voice and it froze Levitz in place. "Drop your ass back in that chair. Don't you get it? I don't *have* much later." Delia glared at the cop until he obediently sat. I hid a smile. Levitz was never that cooperative.

"Stupid goddamned cop," she muttered. "First you're all gangbusters to talk to me, now you want to high-tail it outta here." She settled back against the pillows and pointed shakily at the bedside table. There was a pitcher and an empty glass with a bendy straw sitting there. I filled the glass with water from the pitcher and held the straw to her lips.

She smiled a little and took a few sips, then grimaced. "Nasty stuff, water. Be so much better if someone was to slip some bourbon in it." A few more sips and she waved me off. "Now this don't justify nothin', but Sherm was always having flings of his own. Maybe that's why we lasted so long. We never had no illusions about the other one. One night I come to the coffee shop late. I was always the numbers person, Sherm just never wanted to bother with it, but I hadn't gotten to the shop's books because I'd been out of town on a land deal — a real business trip, mind you. Picked up some property in Indiana that later got turned into an industrial park. Anyways, doin' the books after hours wasn't a problem. I kinda liked being alone in the quiet, only that night, it wasn't so quiet. I kept hearing noises from the back room. That wasn't right. The shop was closed and that part of it was being renovated. I tiptoed back there and peeked in to see Sherm and this blonde rollin' around in the dropcloths. Now I mighta been foolin' around, too, but I done it discrete, y'know. Away from our own place. Well, I yelled at 'em and the woman turns around and damn if it wasn't Jess in drag." Her fingers tightened on the mask, but she didn't lift it from where it lay on the bed.

After a few rasping breaths, she continued, "I didn't take that real good. My face musta been a sight because Jess just laughed and laughed. Honest, I don't remember what happened after that, I just remember comin' to on th' floor with Sherm wrestlin' me for a hammer."

The silence of the room was only broken by the quiet beeps of the medical monitors and Levitz flipping to another page in his notebook. Delia Hammond struggled for breath. fists clenched into the bed clothes. I got the impression she was fighting emotion more than the emphysema.

When she spoke again, her voice was barely

a whisper. "We didn't know what to do. Here we was just gettin' legit and this happens. Stupid goddamned Jess Wynan and his stupid goddamned games. I don't know how long we stood there, me huggin' Sherm and Sherm huggin' me. Then Shem says, 'Who's got to know?' He was right. All our business dealings had been under the table. Nobody knew our relationship with Jess Wynan was more than just the Old Louisville stuff. If anyone knew Jess swung both ways, they wasn't gonna say it — not in '75."

She took a long pull at the oxygen. Levitz waited, pen poised over a new page. I freshened the water and offered it to her. She shook her head and started talking again.

"The whole basement was bein' redone and he was already layin' on a drop cloth. We dragged him down there, dug a hole, dropped him in and covered him up. Later, we found where his wig come off on the stairs, so we tied it to the hammer an' tossed 'em both in the river. Whole place was gettin' a redo then so everything was crazy. Nobody paid no attention to a little dug up dirt or a few missing things."

When she paused, Levitz looked up and asked, "OK, you kept quiet about this all these years; why come clean now? You coulda kept stonewalling us."

Delia snorted, which was a bad move. The snort sent her into a coughing fit that threatened to throw her from the bed. I reached for the nurse call button. She smacked my hand away, snatched the oxygen and sucked air furiously until the attack subsided. At length, she rasped, "You found him, dincha? I'm dyin' anyway, what difference is it gonna make to me? I mean what ya gonna do? Toss me in jail for life? Give me the death penalty? Besides, if I don't own up now, it might cause problems for the kid. She's a little bitch, but I don't want that."

Delia waved her hand petulantly. "I told her not to sell that parcel but does she listen? Not a bit! Don't even bother to consult her old lady about it first. Bet this'll play hob with her high society dreams. I saw this comin' when Sherm set it all up, but he never listened to me, neither. She's tryin' to be too high class for her own good — well, you seen her."

Levitz was gathering his things and not knowing what else to say I replied, "Your daughter is a very beautiful woman."

Delia snorted again, although this time more successfully. She said, "Yeah, looks just like her daddy, does Jessica."

As we left, I could have sworn I heard her mutter, "Dresses like him, too." But I can't swear to it.

Ten

Levitz stomped out and made for the parking lot, punctuating each footfall with a new swearword — it was an impressive vocabulary. I caught up with him at the car. He was leaning against the trunk looking out over the sunrise. He said, "I remember when Jess Wynan turned up missing. It was one of the first cases I worked. At the time, I was surprised at how no one seemed too bent out of shape that he was gone and not all that anxious to get him back. Wonder how many of 'em suspected what really happened?"

"You gonna ask them?"

He dug out the keys and spat, "Hell no! I'll just concentrate on ducking when this goes public."

It was true. Delia's confession left Levitz in an unenviable position. People with different agendas would be screaming at him from all different directions. I wondered if I could drop Dan Ellington on him, too. After all, one good turn deserved another.

He threw himself into the driver's seat, then sat there with a sour look long enough I was getting concerned. Suddenly, he jammed the key into the ignition and growled, "I dunno, though. Seems a little too easy, don't it?"

Right in the middle of a really good dream — an unusual occurrence for me these days — the phone shrilled by my ear. I reached for it and rolled over onto Hoover who took offense and went flying. On the second ring, I answered. It was Levitz. "Powell, get dressed and meet me out at Whispering Oaks."

"Wha. . . ? Levitz, it's four thirty!"

"Yeah. It is. And somebody wasted Delia Hammond and Phyllis Soward mebbe an hour ago."

At Whispering Oaks, the officer at the gate waved me right through with only a slight smirk at the primer polka-dot Pacer. In too short a time I was standing next to Levitz just inside Delia Hammond's room. It looked pretty much the same as it did the last time except for the blood and the fact the two women were sprawled dead, Delia on her bed and Phyllis on the floor. The photogs were shooting the scene from every possible angle and the crime scene people were unloading their gear waiting their turn.

There was a pillow on the floor that looked wrong. I leaned forward for a better view.

Levitz noticed and said, "Looks like that was used as a silencer. Crude, but effective."

I straightened. "This stinks, Levitz."

"Sure does. At least you're out of it."

"Huh?"

"The job for Burgess Insurance. All wrapped up with a big bow on top." Levitz shrugged. "Delia confessed. Now she's dead. No trial, no mess. Later today, you can report to Dan Ellington, pick up your check and move on to something else. Can't say the same for me. Looks like my too easy case just got real hard."

Back home, I slipped several Diana Krall disks into the player, poured myself a dollop of Jameson's and sat in the dark letting the lady sing love songs to me. I hadn't known Phyllis well, but you don't need intimacy to be angry at seeing a person lying on a cold linoleum floor with a neat little hole in her forehead. Poor kid. Here she'd thought she'd found a ride out and ended up on the last one.

Eleven

When the official police report landed on my desk, there was a note from Levitz stuck to the first page. "*In case you decide to buy a canary. L*" I was confused until I read the report itself. It read like a bad thriller. Paid assassination. Organized crime. Give me a break. If they were going to sweep the thing under a rug, they could have at least worked to find a rug that fit. Levitz was right, the best this hunk of verbiage was good for was to line a bird cage.

I printed out my own report and added the still-warm laser pages to the pile, thumping the edges on the desk to even the stack before I slid it into a manila envelope. It looked awfully small sitting in the middle of the blotter. Seemed like the violent death of three human beings should call for more than a dozen pieces of paper.

For a check as large as the one Burgess Insurance was cutting for Trueblood, I usually visit the client myself to hand over a written report in person. Sometimes the client wants a Q&A session, too. Dan Ellington was the kind of detail-oriented guy who wanted a *lot* of Q&A.

Until then, I'd only spoken to Ellington on the phone, he had this booming voice that gave me a mental image of a linebacker. Funny how mental images are so often wrong. In reality, the man was maybe five feet tall and built like a fireplug — very animated fireplug. During the forty-five minutes I spent in his office, I don't think he ever sat still. If he wasn't pacing, he was fiddling with a cigar or shuffling through the pages of the reports. He surprised me again when he suddenly wheeled, jabbed the air with his cigar and demanded, "You don't think this is over, do you, Powell? You think the idea that this was an organized crime hit is bullshit, don't you?"

I didn't see any reason to equivocate. "Yes, sir."

He nodded and huffed cigar smoke. "You're probably right, this just smells like a load of crap." He poked the air with the cigar again. "Still, as far as Burgess Insurance is concerned, this is finished. Deal closed. Any further investigation you do is on your own nickel."

"I'm aware of that, sir."

"HAH! You're going to keep poking the bear, aren't you?" Ellington grinned. "I knew it! I looked into your record when Ray Levitz recommended you, Powell. Liked what I saw. You're a bulldog and aren't about to walk away from a job half-done. Keep me posted, will you? It's got my curiosity up, too, and I'd love to see how it ends."

Ellington was right. I was going to keep poking the bear, I just hadn't told myself, yet. I wasn't sure what kind of stick to use, either, but there was no way I could leave it alone. Some could say Delia Hammond and Jess Wynan had it coming, but Phyllis Soward didn't. They call folks like Phyllis collateral damage.

I call that bullshit.

Twelve

Over the next few days, I tried to shove the murders
to the back burner. It didn't work. The same
questions kept bobbing to the surface. I didn't buy
the public explanation that it was a hit. I knew
Levitz didn't, either. It made no sense. Why after
all these years — and why Phyllis, too? Also, why
be so messy? There were at least a hundred ways
to do it quietly and make no ripples. This way got
everyone's attention.

In my career with the FBI, I'd investigated
all kinds of hits and gut instinct told me this was
amateur night. It was more like someone trying
to make it look like the made-for-TV version of a
mob killing more than the real thing. Something
else was working here, too — something below
the surface. Damn me if I could figure out what it
was. Finally, I headed over to Sandy's office and
set him to ferreting out everything he could on
Delia and Sherm Hammond, Jess Wynan, the
Wynan Old Louisville Trust and the two families

in general. It won me a skeptical look, but there wasn't much else doing, so he agreed. I confess I didn't expect much.

It was probably Sandy's idea of revenge for dropping a non-paying job on him, but he marched into my office just at quitting time and plunked a huge stack of printouts on my desk. Didn't bother me in the least. Having something to read and mull over might take my mind off the stark red on white images imprinted on my mind at Whispering Oaks.

My hopes for the research were too high. Some of it was the same stuff I'd seen in Levitz' file. Most of it was the dry fact of names, dates and the like. The few newspaper stories were a nice break, but still didn't fill any blanks. I really hit paydirt with the photographs, though it wasn't the paydirt I was expecting. Delia had once been a very beautiful woman and had dressed accordingly. I imagine it would have been a sort of shock to hear that foghorn voice coming out of that glamorous mouth.

Sherm, on the other hand, looked like a stereotypical hoodlum. If he'd gone to Hollywood, he could have made a pretty solid living playing sinister muscle in TV shows. No speaking parts, just looming. I was amused recalling Delia's comment that Jessica looked just like her father until I found a picture of Jess Wynan and got a real jolt. I also suddenly understood Delia's muttered comments as Levitz and I were leaving.

Jess. Jessica. What an idiot I'd been to miss that — although it looked like a lot of other people had either missed it or ignored it. Then again, according to Delia, no one knew about her relationship to Wynan. So who'd even be looking?

Thirteen

An even bigger stack of printouts graced my desk the next morning. Sandy had outdone himself and I settled in to read. On the top were new pieces from the Louisville, Lexington and Frankfort newspapers. With a decades-old mystery solved and a new, sensational chapter to add, they'd gone at it with enthusiasm. People were coming out of the woodwork to tell their version of things — all except the Wynan family. They'd lawyered up as soon as Jess was identified and hadn't said boo after the first statement of shock, grief and certainty the police would close the case to satisfaction. Uh huh.

There were stories highlighting Sherm and Delia's shady past with pictures of them with both the famous and infamous of the day. Prominent people expressed dismay that a businessman of Jess Wynan's caliber could have been hoodwinked into the schemes. There were statements from and interviews with people high and low. The low were frequently small-time hoods who had dealt with the Hammonds. The high were just as frequently people in positions of influence disavowing any relationship with Wynan and swearing ignorance of either real estate swindles or alternative sexual practices. There was even one analysis of the present day real estate market as compared to that of the 1970s, although Sandy probably included that one out of pure meanness. All-in-all, it made some very interesting reading.

Later, I was sipping coffee and mulling it all over when the phone in the outer office rang. A wide-eyed Wanda appeared in the doorway. She fidgeted for a moment before she whispered, "It's Jessica Hammond on line one. What do you want me to do?"

I nearly choked on the coffee. "I'll take it." Wanda disappeared gratefully. I lifted the phone and punched the lit-up button.

After a lengthy conversation with Miss Jessica, I headed to Sandy's office and leaned in the door-way. Leaning in was easier than trying to fight my way into it. With all the technology crammed into that small space, it was a miracle there was room for Sandy. I said, "Hey! Looks like you might get paid for your Hammond research after all."

He popped up from behind a twenty-eight-inch flat panel monitor. "Yeah?"

"I just talked to Jessica Hammond. She's hiring us to look into the murders."

"And you said 'no,' right?"

"If I'd said no, how would we get paid?"

He whistled. "Man, Levitz is gonna hate this."

"Are you kidding? He told her to call."

My first nighttime glimpse of the Hammond place hadn't done it justice. I rang the doorbell and looked it over while waiting on the doorstep. It was a beautiful place, limestone with white trim set in a rolling, snow-covered lawn. Professionally trimmed shrubs poked through the layer of white all along the freshly plowed driveway. Jessica Hammond opened the door, herself. The lady was much cooler than the first encounter. She only frowned slightly at the wreck I'd parked in front of her house beautiful.

I shrugged at the car. "Honda's in the shop. Getting a loaner can be a crapshoot."

She nodded vaguely, then stepped back from the door offering me an impressive view of both the lady and the elegant foyer beyond. She said, "Mr. Powell, I'm glad you could come over so quickly."

As she lead me farther into the house, I was even more impressed and mildly surprised. After Delia and Jessica's brassy outburst that first night, I maybe expected tiger skin rugs and velvet Elvis paintings, instead, the place was a photo spread from *Architectural Digest*. Someone had either a hidden talent for interior decorating or the sense to hire a professional one.

Jessica, herself, was different, too. All trace of the shrill anger I'd heard when I was there with Levitz was gone. Today, her voice was pitched lower and reeked of sultry promise and professional coaching. I wondered if her mother had done something similar. She closed the door and said, "I hope you don't mind, but Terry Newman insisted on being here this morning, too."

I shrugged. "Why should I mind if your lawyer is present?"

She looked uncomfortable. "Terry is a little more than just my lawyer — at least he wants to be."

"You don't sound as sure."

She smiled suddenly. "The study is this way, Mr. Powell."

I was confused until I turned to follow and saw Newman standing in the door of what must be the study. He didn't look happy, but I wouldn't know, I'd never seen him look any other way.

Outwardly Jessica was relaxed and casual in slacks and shirttails, but I could tell she was wired. Newman didn't give way when we approached. It was a double door, but he was a big guy and stood in our way like a tanned and manicured Border Guard. "I want to state up front that I think there's no reason to hire a Private Investigator to second-guess the police. It's a waste of money."

"Good thing it's *my* money hiring him, then." She hardly slowed as she brushed past him. He made it harder for me to get by and we stood nose-to-nose glaring like good little Neanderthals until Jessica snapped, "*Terry!*"

She shook her head and made for a large desk carved from some dark wood that stood by a set of French doors. Pulling a cigarette out of an alabaster box next to an ashtray full of crushed butts, she tapped it on the desktop and lit it. As if she'd read my mind, she said, "Macho bullshit. Honestly, it's a miracle either one of you manages words bigger than ug."

Newman stopped staring daggers at me and turned them on her. "Jessica, dear, you're smoking way too much these days."

"I always smoke when I'm nervous, *darling*."

"You know I'm only concerned for your health, Jessie. Both your father and mother. . . ."

Her cheeks reddened and I doubted it was from embarrassment. I expected her to blow, but she just took a deeper drag and returned his stare. "Emphysema didn't take either of my parents. Daddy died in a car crash and Mother took bullet in the head, which is why Mr. Powell is here." She shot a stream of smoke into the air. "Don't you have a client to meet or something?"

Ouch. And people thought the threat of nuclear annihilation was a thing of the past. I was glad I was still in the hall with an unobstructed path to the exit.

Newman blinked first. He glanced at his Rolex. "Good God, Jessie, you're right. I was supposed to be there ten minutes ago." He strode across the room to give her a peck of a kiss, then headed past me toward the door, calling over his shoulder, "I'll phone you later this evening."

I wished I could have been there when he saw the polka-dot Pacer. I said, "Happy guy."

"He's a control freak." She viciously stubbed out the cigarette and snorted derisively, sounding remarkably like the late Delia. "Compared to Mother, he's a featherweight."

"At the risk of vaporization, I have to point out that Mr. Newman may be right. I might not be able to turn up anything more than the police did."

"Maybe, but this isn't only about the murders it's . . . related — well probably related . . . oh hell. It'll be easier to show you." Without another word, she headed out through the French doors into the cold, gray day. I paused long enough to allow myself one soundless whistle, then followed, glad I hadn't shucked my coat.

What passed for a backyard in Jessica's neck of the woods was a walled snow-covered garden filled with statuary, small fountains and formal paths lined with evenly spaced urns of plants. Well, what were *once* evenly spaced urns of plants. Every urn had been smashed to bits on the flagstones of the path. The supporting columns had been shoved over and holes dug where they'd stood. Holes also dotted the flowerbeds, and in several places, stones were gouged out of the garden wall. An attempt at cleanup had been made. Much of the debris had been swept up or collected into piles, but it must have been a disaster area before.

Jessica continued a distance until she came to what looked like an old abbey archway flanked by two glassless quatrefoil windows. It was covered in cold-blackened ivy everywhere except where two pedestals had been overturned. Red marble vases that must have once sat on the pedestals were smashed across a badly damaged stone bench and jagged remains poked up through the snow like bloodied teeth. She stopped and gestured at the wreckage. "This happened the night after Mother and Ms. Soward were killed while I was in town talking with Lt. Levitz."

"Geez! What did the police say about it?"

"I didn't call the police."

"You didn't — why the hell not?"

She studied me a long time before she answered. "I don't trust the police, Mr. Powell. Maybe it's something I inherited from my parents. I know they started off as petty criminals. Oh, they did their best to keep me from finding out: expensive boarding schools and all that. Still, I heard the rumors. Heard my friend's parents whispering. Anyway, I found out. I also figured that it didn't matter to me."

"Until now. You think all this is related to your parent's past?"

"Yes! What else could it be? My mother confesses to an ancient murder; suddenly, she and an innocent nurse are dead and someone is tearing the home I inherited from my parents apart. Do you have an other explanation?"

She had a point, but before I could say that, she sank down on the damaged bench and whispered, "I still can't believe my mother actually *killed* someone. I knew she was a hardass, but. . . ?" She fumbled a pack of cigarettes out of her slacks pocket and put one in her mouth. Her hands shook so badly when she tried to light it, I took the lighter away and did it for her.

"Maybe it's no consolation, but I was there when she confessed. She didn't plan to kill Wynan. She didn't even remember doing it. It's probably true, Levitz will tell you the same thing: people in extreme situations lose control and do violent things." I watched her take several shaky drags off the cigarette and wondered if she'd figured out that it was her biological father that her mother killed. I didn't ask, though. It wasn't the time or the place. It might not even have been relevant. I said, "Look, you really ought to call Levitz. . . ."

"JEEZUZ! Once a cop always a cop, huh? I told you. I don't want them involved."

I didn't bother to mention it was too late. Murder has a way of getting cops involved. I said, "OK. What do you want me to do?"

"I want you to find out who's doing this. I'm scared, Mr. Powell. I don't want to end up like Mother and Phyllis Soward."

There it was. I waited for more.

She stubbed the cigarette out on the abused bench, stood and started back toward the house.

"The Coroner has released my mother's body, so her funeral is tomorrow and then I have to go out of town for a few days. Boston."

"What for?"

"Something Terry set up. A real estate deal that's a sign now or forever regret not doing it." She sighed. "If you want the truth, I'd rather not go. I hate the hassle flying has become, but business is business and with the way the market is now, I can't afford to blow this off."

"And you're thinking it's a perfect opportunity for someone wanting to trash the place."

"Exactly."

She led me back into the house. I was glad, I was half-frozen. She had to be, too, but you couldn't tell from looking. She went over to the desk and she pulled a check out of the drawer. Handing it to me, she said, "I made this out right after we spoke this morning."

The check was made out for the standard Trueblood retainer. She'd done her research well. Accepting the check was accepting the case. I took it and folded it into my pocket. "First thing, I'll need a tour of the house. I want to see what your security situation is.

Fourteen

Jessica Hammond was right: once a cop always a cop even if that cop was a Fed. My first stop on the way back to the office was to Levitz' office. Color me surprised when he was actually glad to see me. He didn't want to talk at the station, though, and soon we were sitting in a back booth at a local deli.

"Glad the Hammond girl called you, Powell. This thing is gonna be a shit shower and she's caught in the middle of it."

"Which brings me to 'why,' Levitz."

"Because this business of a mob hit is crap — but you know that already."

"Cover-up?"

"Nah. Just someone looking for a quick fix to an inconvenient problem."

"Helluva way to describe a murder."

Levitz just nodded and ripped two sugars and two Sweet'N'Lows into his tea.

I tried not to look at the sludge in the bottom of his glass. "So it's been shelved?"

"Not exactly, but it isn't a high priority for the department. Now it's your turn. What did the kid ask you to do?"

"Come on. Levitz, you know I can't tell you that after taking a retainer."

He tossed his napkin at the table in frustration. "Dammit, Powell! Then why make the social call?" He growled, snatched another napkin and attacked his sandwich.

I took a slow pull on my Mexican hot chocolate and let the warmth seep through me. "I *can* tell you what anyone who looks into the back yard of her home could see, though. Someone trashed the place the night after Delia Hammond and Phyllis Soward were killed."

He stopped chewing and gulped down the mouthful. "Trashed? Like how?"

"Like digging holes, knocking down stone fences and smashing decorative urns. Like maybe looking for something? Your turn again. Any idea what someone might go through all that effort to find?"

He didn't answer immediately, but went back to munching. I might as well not have been there for the next few minutes, he was far away rummaging through the file cabinets in his head. Fine by me. I had a lot of spicy chocolate left.

When he came back he said, "Mind, I don't know specifics, but there might be somethin'. When Jess Wynan disappeared, there was rumors that a lot of cash did, too. Mebbe another reason no one thought he mighta been murdered. Everyone thought he was gonna turn up in South America or somethin'."

"Money was missing, too? Seems like that would turn the heat up on a case, not down."

"Someone has to press charges or file somethin' first. You were a fed; you know the red tape dance. The Wynan family filed a Missing Person report, then gave marginal co-operation."

"No corpse, no murder."

"Yep."

When Levitz heard that Jessica was going out of town right after the funeral, he swore a blue streak. The man is a true artist. He is also a true cop. "Geez flippin' Louise! Somebody busts up her yard and she flits off and leaves the house empty right after? She leave a spare key in the mailbox, too?"

I shrugged. "Seems screwed up to me, too. Some kind of business trip that she can't get out of apparently. Her lawyer is insisting she goes."

"Terry Ratsass Newman. Got me in a world of hurt with the brass. Shoulda give in to the impulse to rearrange his face when we was freezin' our asses off in that driveway. Might have gotten me in more trouble, but it would have been gratifying."

"You're gonna love this, then. Newman's moving in on little miss Hammond."

He loved it. After a fresh burst of profanity, he said, "Oh well, that's the rich for you, ain't it? No skin off my nose either way." He examined his sandwich, splorted more brown mustard on it and took another big bite. After a moment, he said, "Well, the least we can to is up the patrols on the neighborhood. Keep an eye on the place while she's gone. Whoever trashed the garden has to be connected to the shootings. Doesn't make sense otherwise."

I nodded and turned my attention to my own sandwich. Might be a good idea for me to put in a little patrol time there, myself.

Fifteen

The following day was taken up with funerals. I put in my appearance at Delia's, ignored glares from Terry Newman, reassured Jessica I was on the job, then went to Phyllis'. There weren't many people there, just a sister and her elderly mother. The forgotten victim. It seemed to help that I came, so I stayed and rode with them to the cemetery in the rented limo.

I spent that night in my car, alternately tooling past the Hammond place and warming up over coffee in one of the many restaurants not far away. It wasn't like I could sleep, anyway. I'd been plagued by nightmares ever since the murder. Thank you, PTSD.

I was sitting in one of those restaurants when my cell went off. It was Jessica Hammond.

"Mr. Powell, I need you here right away."

"In *Boston?*"

"There's a snowstorm between here and Boston, so my fight was canceled. I took a taxi home from the airport . . . there's someone moving around downstairs." Her voice was pitched so low, it was hard to hear, but there was no mistaking the fear in it.

"Ms. Hammond. . . ."

"Mr. Powell, this isn't a come-on. I can come up with better lines than this if I want sex. There's someone in the house. I'm — locked in my bedroom."

I didn't ask why she had locks on her bedroom door. "Call the cops, this is what they're there for."

"No."

"OK, *I'll* call them."

"NO! I don't want the cops!"

She was either a first-class actress or she was scared down to her toes. I relented and though the snowstorm that closed the East coast airports was moving into Louisville, pushed the Pacer to its limits to get there in record time.

I tried to be a quiet as possible as I pulled into the drive, but the Pacer was loud and cold air is a good sound conductor. Whoever was in the house heard me and as I came through the side gate, he was pelting across the garden.

Training kicked in and before I knew it, I was in pursuit. He vaulted over the stone wall at the back of the property and I followed, but when I dropped down, I hit a slick incline and went sliding into a snow-covered drainage ditch. With my gimped legs, there was no way to halt the slide and by the time I got myself out, my guy was nowhere to be seen. There was, however, the sound of a car engine starting up and receding in the distance. I leaned against a tree to catch my breath and tried to decide if I was sorry I didn't catch up with him.

Sixteen

By the time I limped around to the front door, the snow that gotten into my clothes during the slide was melting. I punched her number into the cell and when she picked up, asked, "You on a cordless phone?"

"Yes."

"Good. I'm at the front door. Stay on as you come down."

"I'm in the hall already."

"Keep talking. I think the guy is gone, but I don't want to take any chances."

A light went on inside. "Geez, the study is trashed!"

"Don't stop and look!"

"OK, OK! I'm at the door."

She peeked through a sidelight and let me in with visible relief as she thumbed the phone off. "You look awful, what happened?"

"Your visitor and I went walking in the winter wonderland."

"Looks more like a sleigh ride without the sleigh. Let me get you something warm to drink."

"Later. Right now I want to make sure there's no one in the house but us."

"I'm coming with you. I'll know if anything has been messed with, you won't."

We made a quick circuit of the house and aside from the study being a mess, the only other worrying thing was that the alarm system was turned off. Not disabled. Off. She stared at it and went pale. "I'm sure I turned that back on when I got home. After what's been happening . . . I'm *sure*."

I believed her, but didn't like the way my thoughts were running. We turned it back on, then went to the kitchen where she insisted on making me a cup of cocoa. I was dripping by that time and said as long as there was also a towel involved, she had a deal.

In the kitchen, she tossed me a towel, and amazed me by putting a pan of milk on the stove and pulling out real cocoa powder. She saw my raised eyebrows and laughed. "One of the boarding schools my parents sent me to had an emphasis on domestic things. If I didn't get anything else out of it, I learned my way around a kitchen." She deftly whipped the cocoa and sugar into the heating milk. "Besides that instant stuff just doesn't taste as good."

She was right, I sipped the cocoa and appreciated the rich flavor almost as much as the warm mug against my cold hands.

Jessica leaned against the counter and lit one of her omnipresent cigarettes. She blew smoke and observed, "You don't like me much, do you, Mr. Powell?"

"That's not what I'm being paid for."

"Oh, that costs extra?"

I grinned. "No, that's a perk."

She grinned back. "Terry says you're some kind of hero."

I got back to sipping cocoa. Just didn't want to go there. She wasn't deterred, though. "He says you got a commendation from the President and everything."

Finally, I said, "Having a building dropped on you doesn't make you a hero. Just ask the Wicked Witch of the East."

"Very good, Powell. Glad to know you don't consider yourself a hero because heroes do stupid things and we wouldn't want that." That came from the hall. We turned toward the voice and Terry Newman. After we'd found the alarm turned off, I'd expected that. He had a gun pointed at us.

I'd expected that, too. Sometimes I just hate being right.

Jessica glared at him. She was too smart for the "what are you doing here" bit. She caught on real fast. Instead she said, "Is that the same gun you shot Mother with?"

The question seemed to make him angrier. "Where's the 'cookie jar,' Jessica?"

"What?" She looked genuinely confused. "I don't understand."

I'd been edging away from Newman to make it harder for him to cover both of us. Jessica noticed, but he didn't. He was too focused on her. Fine. It let me make a slow move toward the weapon I kept clipped to my belt.

"Don't play dumb with me, Bitch," He snarled. "I know better. Your parents were skimming money off the real estate deals with Wynan and converting it to gold. You know where they hid it. Your father told me so."

She was even more confused and afraid, but not losing control. She backed against the kitchen cabinet leaning against it for support. "I don't know what you're talking about, Terry. Why would Daddy tell you something like that?"

"Because he thought it was a joke! Because he liked to jerk people around — liked to jerk *me* around. Two-bit hood. Just because he made money, he thought he was better than the rest of us. He kept making comments about having plenty stashed away for a rainy day. Thought he was being obscure, but I did my homework. I knew there was money missing after Wynan disappeared. A lot of money."

Newman's voice had been rising in volume throughout his monologue. He waved the pistol and screamed, "Where is it?"

Jessica pressed against the counter, fear on her face.

He closed in on her, shouting, "He said he put it in Jessica's Cookie Jar! Where is it?"

Everything happened all at once. Jessica's hand closed on the handle of the hot cocoa pot and she brought it around against the hand holding the pistol. Newman screamed and fired a wild shot into the wall as I brought my stun gun up into the side of his neck and pressed the trigger. He jerked and dropped as the kitchen filled with police.

Levitz holstered his pistol. "Somebody cuff that sonuvabitch and read him his rights when he stops twitching."

When I could breathe again, I snapped, "Think you could cut it a little closer next time, Levitz?"

"Dunno. There gonna be a next time, Powell? You could have been a little quicker, yourself and called us *before* you chased the perp off and lost him in the snow."

Seventeen

Dawn found us back in a cemetery — all of us except Terry Newman. He was all snug in the downtown jail awaiting his day in court. Jessica fidgeted beside me and toyed with her cigarette case as we watched the police and assorted officials open the Wynan family crypt at Cave Hill Cemetery with a key from Delia Hammond's personal key ring. I think she'd forgiven me by then for calling Levitz before I called her to come to the door. Maybe.

She suddenly said, "I hadn't thought of this place in years. We used to come here for picnics when I was a kid. It all makes sense now, doesn't it?"

"What does?"

"Why this place, this crypt?" She quirked a smile at me. "Yeah. I finally figured that out, too. Mother always used to say I looked just like my father then laugh like it was the biggest joke. Guess it was."

The hinges on the big bronze door didn't make a sound as they swung back.

She stood on tiptoe to see over the knot of cops as the blocked the crypt entrance. "Anyway, when I was maybe four, I went up to the gate and looked in. There was this huge urn on a pedestal under the stained glass window. I asked my parents why dead people needed a cookie jar. They laughed, but I guess they never forgot it."

"Made a pretty good codeword, didn't it?"

"I wonder why they never told me?"

From inside the crypt we heard the sound of stone on stone then Levitz' unmistakable "Holy shit!" The officials reappeared at the door carrying bags that clinked. *Lots* of bags that clinked.

"They intended to. They left a sealed envelope to be opened after they died with the family lawyer telling you where it was. Even there, they only said cookie jar."

"The family lawyer. Terry Newman. Creep — and he really thought Mother would tell the authorities about the gold? *Mother?*"

"Well, she confessed to murdering her partner in the frauds," I said. "He was frantic when that happened, figuring it was only a matter of time before someone else discovered the same information he did."

She was silent for a long time, watching the cops photograph the gleaming contents of the bags. At length, she said, "He was going to kill me, too, wasn't he?"

"He hasn't admitted that yet, but it seems likely. After all, he believed you knew all about the stash and were just playing it cool."

"And I was giving him the shove." Her hands were shaking again as she tried to light her cigarette. As before, I took the lighter and lit it for her.

When I handed it back, she laughed and said, "If this were a movie, we'd look into each other's eyes, then kiss and walk off together." She gazed up at me for a beat, then did her Delia snort. "Not hardly."

We settled for a handshake and the rest of Trueblood's fee.

About the Author

T. Lee Harris is a writer and illustrator. A graduate of Indiana University with a bachelor of fine arts, Harris has put her degree to good use when designing and publishing the *Indian Creek Anthology* series for the Southern Indiana Writers Group and the *Not From Around Here* anthology for the Cincinnati Writers Project.

Several novels are in the works with settings ranging from ancient Egypt to modern-day Chicago.